The House
That Jack Built

Randolph Caldecott

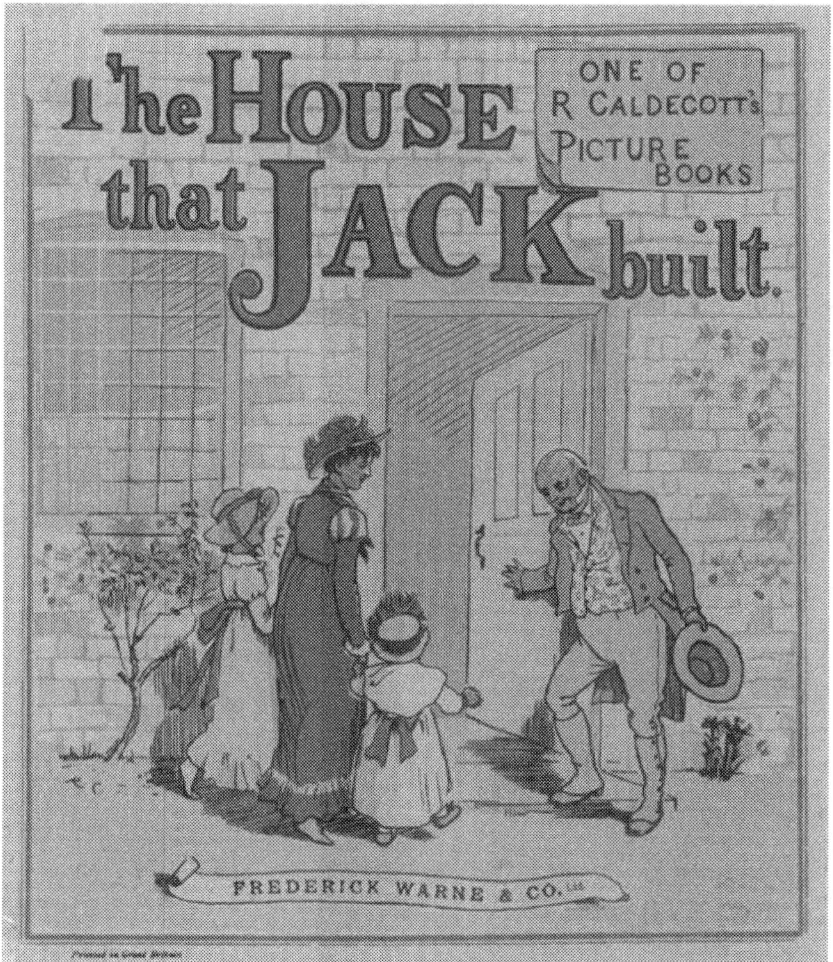
The HOUSE that JACK built.
ONE OF R CALDECOTT's PICTURE BOOKS
FREDERICK WARNE & CO. Ltd
Printed in Great Britain

This is the House that Jack built.

This is the Malt,
That lay in the House that Jack built.

This is the Rat,
That ate the Malt,
That lay in the House that Jack built.

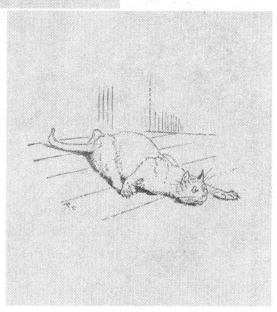

This is the Cat,
That killed the Rat,
That ate the Malt,
That lay in the House that Jack built.

This is the Dog,
That worried the Cat,
That killed the Rat,
That ate the Malt,
That lay in the House that Jack built.

This is the Cow with the crumpled horn,

That tossed the Dog,
That worried the Cat,
That killed the Rat,
That ate the Malt,
That lay in the House that
    Jack built.

This is the Maiden all forlorn,
That milked the Cow with the crumpled horn,

That tossed the Dog,
That worried the Cat,
That killed the Rat,
That ate the Malt,
That lay in the House
that Jack built.

This is the Man all tattered and torn,
That kissed the Maiden all forlorn,

That milked the Cow with
    the crumpled horn,
That tossed the Dog,
That worried the Cat,
That killed the Rat,
That ate the Malt,
That lay in the House
    that Jack built.

This is the Priest, all shaven and shorn,
That married the Man all tattered and torn,
That kissed the Maiden all forlorn,

That milked the Cow with
the crumpled horn,
That tossed the Dog,
That worried the Cat,
That killed the Rat,
That ate the Malt,
That lay in the House that
Jack built.

This is the Cock that crowed in the morn
That waked the Priest all shaven and shorn,
That married the Man all tattered and torn,
That kissed the Maiden all forlorn,

That milked the Cow with
    the crumpled horn,
That tossed the Dog,
That worried the Cat,
That killed the Rat,
That ate the Malt,
That lay in the House that
    Jack built.

This is the Farmer who sowed the corn,
That fed the Cock that crowed in the morn,
That waked the Priest all shaven and shorn,
That married the Man all tattered and torn,
That kissed the Maiden all forlorn,
That milked the Cow with the crumpled horn,

That tossed the Dog,
That worried the Cat,
That killed the Rat,
That ate the Malt,
That lay in the House
   that Jack built.

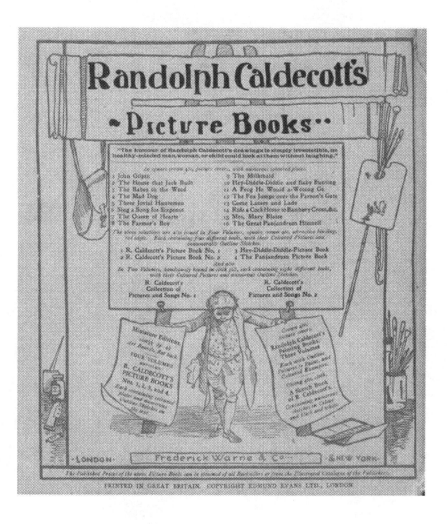